CATCH THAT TIRE!

Adapted by Eric Geron

Based on the episode "A Wheel Good Time"
by Jordan Gershowitz

Published by Mattel Press, 333 Continental Boulevard, El Segundo, CA 90245.

No part of this book may be reproduced or transmitted in any form or by any means, electronic or mechanical, including photocopying, recording, or by any information storage and retrieval system, without written permission from the publisher. For more information, please visit the Trademark & Copyright section at https://corporate.mattel.com/contact-us.

ISBN 9781683432227
10 9 8 7 6 5 4 3 2 1
This edition first printing, May 2024
Printed in China QP
Visit us at Mattel.com.

This is Coop.

He loves cars.

He wants to race them.

2

This is Coop's dad.

He knows Coop can be a racer.

Dash runs a racing camp.

She will teach Coop.

There are other kids at camp too.

The camp is in the Ultimate Garage.

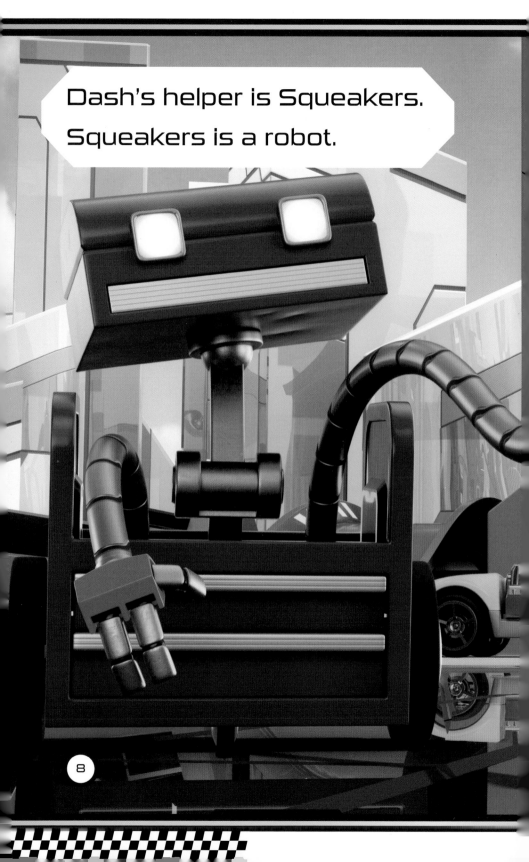

Dash's helper is Squeakers. Squeakers is a robot.

He will show them something cool.

Look at all the cars!
Each one has a special power.
The kids will pick cars to race.
Which cars will they choose?

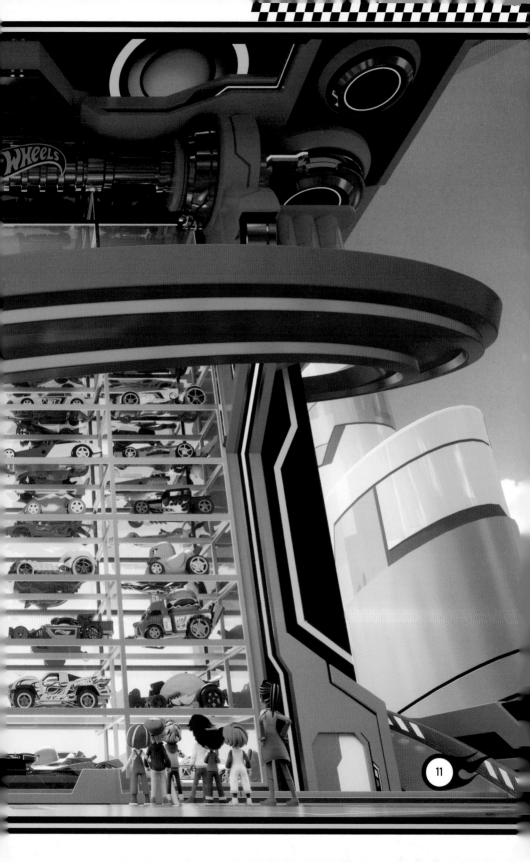

The campers get cool racing gloves.

They will use the gloves to drive.

Uh-oh!

Coop bumps into a tire.

It flies out the window.

Someone could get hurt.

Coop feels bad.

He wants to fix his mistake.

His new friends will help him.

Challenge accepted!

Brights turns on the Track Builder.

It is a machine.

It will help find the tire.

Coop needs a car.

He needs one that is fast.

Coop races to catch the tire.

But part of the track is missing.
Coop is going to fall!

Axle is using the Track Builder.

He is erasing the track!

But Coop knows what to do.

His car has a special power.

Go, Hot Wheels!

The car zooms over the big gap.

Can it land safely?

Yes!

Coop catches the tire.

Wow!

His friends are happy.

Coop is a great racer!

He chose a great car.

Coop tells Dash about the tire.

She is glad he got it back.

Coop did not give up.

He fixed his mistake.

He had help along the way.

It is time to race again.

Which cars should they choose?

Challenge accepted!